The Duck Who Flew Upside Down

Written by Russ Towne

Illustrated by Josh McGill

Books for Young Children

V. G. and Dexter Dufflebee

The Grumpadinkles

Ki-Gra's REALLY, REALLY BIG Day!

The Duck Who Flew Upside Down

Clyde and Friends

Clyde and Hoozy Whatzadingle

Clyde and I Help a Hippo to Fly

Rusty Bear and Thomas Too

Clyde and I

Children's App
Based on Characters from the Clyde Books

Clyde and Friends children's app developed by Gail Nelson
using characters from Russ's series of Clyde books:

www.ClydeandFriends.com

Dedication

This book is dedicated to my wife Heidi for being my faithful life partner, friend, sounding board, confidant, and much more, through thick and thin, for over 34 years. Thank you for who and what you are to me, and for your expert and patient feedback regarding my ideas for children's books.

Acknowledgments

Thank you to my family and friends for all the ways you brighten my life.

Special thanks to:

Josh McGill for being such a great illustrator, and for being easy to work with, patient, helpful, professional, someone who keeps his word, and meets deadlines.

Denis Loiseau for inviting me to co-write songs with him and in so doing became the spark that lit my creative candle.

Adrian Bedard for creating the video that helped launch my Kickstarter funding campaign.

Sue and Ian Stevens for always being there when it counts the most.

Polly Letofsky for your advice, encouragement, and information regarding book publishing.

Gail Nelson for your excellent book layout and cover design.

Sandy Lardinois for your quick and terrific editing.

For your excellent feedback regarding my story and character ideas, and support and friendship (in alphabetical order):

Mimi Krumholz
Ute Lark
Diane Rawn
Ben Towne

For your continued support and friendship (in alphabetical order):

Patricia Donaghe
Tom Feasby
Kristi Kivi Frimpong
Scott Schroeder
Diana Schwenk

Thank you. I'm eternally grateful.

With Love,
Russ

Wilbur Mallard was a very odd duck.
Although he walked and talked like a duck,
he didn't look like any other duck.

The other ducks in the Mallard flock
had handsome shiny green heads
or were mostly brown.

Not Wilbur!
He was bright orange.
With purple spots.

He also had a great big bright purple
thingamajig on top of his head.

That thingamajig caused a big problem
for Wilbur. Every time he tried to fly,
it turned him upside down.

He tried to fly right-side up,
but every time, he ended up upside down.

Landing was a big problem
for Wilbur, too.
He tried different ways to land
while flying upside down,
but nothing worked.

When he tried to land in fields,
he ended up bouncing, somersaulting, and
finally crashing in a heap.

Landing on water was softer than fields,
but he still bounced and somersaulted.
Instead of a big crash, his water landings
ended with a big splash.

Ducks aren't built to fly upside down.
Wilbur had to work much harder
than the other ducks to fly.

No matter how hard he tried,
he couldn't keep up with the flock
and fell behind.

One day, he got left so far behind
that he never found his flock again.

Wilbur was sad and lonely
but kept on flying.
He loved the warmth from the sun
on his belly feathers.

He heard a voice call from behind.
He turned and saw the most beautiful duck he
had ever seen.

She quacked, "Hi, I'm Eileen."

He was so nervous he could hardly quack.
"H-H-I. I'm, uh, I'm Wilbur."

"I'm pleased to meet you,"
she quacked back.
"Why are you flying upside down and
all alone with such a sad look on your face?"

After Wilbur explained, Eileen said,
"I'm sorry that happened.
If you don't mind,
I'd be happy to fly with you."

19

"Really? That would be great!"
Wilbur quacked excitedly.
"But, aren't you afraid to fly with someone
who looks so funny and flies upside down?
I know I'm a very odd duck."

Eileen said, "You *are* different,
but that's one of the things I like about you.
Most ducks look alike and fly alike.
They are so boring. You are special
because you *aren't* like all the rest."

Wilbur smiled. He had never
thought about it like that before.

As they flew along,
they saw a couple of old ducks
flying all alone.

They told Wilbur and Eileen that
they were too old to keep up
with their Pintail Duck flock.
They had decided to try to make it
on their own so they wouldn't
slow the younger ones down.

Wilbur and Eileen invited the old couple
to join them.
They weren't flying very fast either.
So, the pair of ducks became a flock of four.

As the sun set, they decided to look
for a place to sleep for the night.

They landed near a pair of geese.
Well, the others did.
Wilbur hit the nearby water, bounced,
somersaulted, and landed with a big splash.

Everybody introduced themselves.
Ms. Snow Goose honked,
"Earlier today a big, mean-looking coyote
almost had us for dinner!
We flew away just in time."

The ducks invited the geese to join them.
They agreed that it would be safer
if they stuck together.

They would not be able to sleep
with the hungry coyote nearby
but were too tired to fly much further.

Wilbur quacked an idea to them
and they decided to try it.

The full moon shined brightly
on Mr. Snow Goose.
He was limping in a big field,
pretending to be hurt.

The coyote saw him and
began running toward the goose.

But Mr. Snow Goose's new friends
were ready for the coyote.
They had made a big net out of vines
and dropped it on him.

The coyote was running so fast
he got tangled up in the net
and rolled like a big ball.
He crashed into a tree.
THUD!

They wound vines around his snout
so he couldn't bite or move.

"Now we can get a good night's sleep,"
Wilbur quacked.
And, so they did--everyone but
the hungry coyote.

In the morning, they dragged him
to the edge of a very steep cliff
and took the vines off his snout.

The coyote cried, "Please don't roll me off
that cliff. I promise not to eat you."

They knew they would never really be safe
with a hungry coyote around,
but they didn't want to hurt him.
So, they carefully lowered him by vines
all the way to the bottom of the cliff.

He untangled himself from the net
and ran away as fast as he could.
That was the last they ever saw
of the coyote.

Eileen said, "Let's pull the empty net
back up. We can use it
to protect ourselves again.
And, I have an idea that I think
Wilbur is going to love."

The next time Wilbur tried to land,
he didn't bounce, somersault,
crash, or splash!
His friends had caught him
in the air with the net.

With a little practice, he was even able to
spring off the net and land on his feet.

Word spread about this special flock.
Animals that liked to eat birds heard what
happened to the coyote and stayed away.

Many more birds joined the flock.
Soon baby birds began to hatch.

Some of Wilbur and Eileen's ducklings
looked like him, some looked like her,
and some were brown, orange and purple
all mixed together.
But they all had a bright purple
thingamajig on top of their heads.

Wilbur and Eileen knew their group
had become something so much
greater than a flock.

They had become a family.

The End

CPSIA information can be obtained
at www.ICGtesting.com
Printed in the USA
BVHW02*1438210218
508120BV00018B/126/P